Tick
Tick
DING
DONG!
Tick.
Tick
Tick!
DONG
DONG!

First published in 1983 by Octopus Books Limited
59 Grosvenor Street, London W.1.

This edition published in 1984 by Gallery Books
An imprint of W.H. Smith Publishers Inc.
112 Madison Avenue, New York,
New York 10016

ISBN 0 8317 7512 2

Printed in Hong Kong

ROUND-THE-CLOCK STORIES

KENNETH GRAY

Illustrated by
COLIN HAWKINS

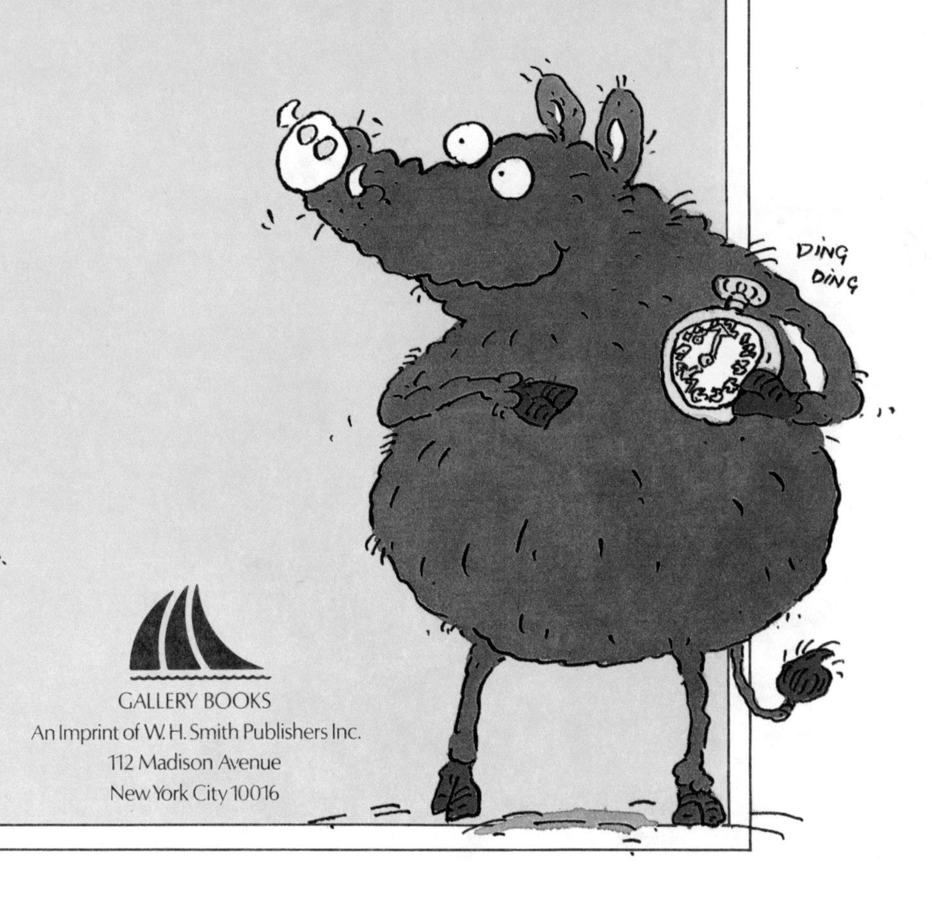

GALLERY BOOKS
An Imprint of W. H. Smith Publishers Inc.
112 Madison Avenue
New York City 10016

The Man The Boy and The Donkey.

Once upon a time a father and his son were going to market with their donkey to buy some supplies for their farm. The father led the donkey and the boy walked by its side.

As they walked down a country lane they passed an old man who looked at them and said, 'Fools! Why is one of you not riding the donkey? That's what donkeys are for after all.'

So the father put his son on the donkey and they went on their way. They had not gone very far when they passed an old lady who said, 'You should be ashamed of yourself riding the donkey while your poor father walks along in the heat of the midday sun.' So the boy got off the donkey's back, and the father mounted the animal.

They set off again. But they had not covered many yards when they saw an old couple sitting in the shade enjoying their simple lunch. 'Look,' said the man to the woman. 'Is it not shameful that that lazy lout sits on the donkey while his son walks alongside.'

Well, the man had no idea what to do. He had been criticized for allowing the donkey to walk along with no one on its back. He had been condemned for riding it while his son walked, and his son had been criticized for riding the animal while the father walked. He thought and thought. At last he realized what he should do. Both his son and he could ride on the donkey's back, and then everyone would be happy. So he pulled his son up and rode into town.

When they arrived at the town people pointed at them and jeered. 'Look! That poor animal is loaded down with the weight of that fat farmer and his loutish son,' they shouted. 'They ought to be ashamed of themselves.'

The man and the boy got off and both of them tried to think what to do. They thought and they thought, till at last they got hold of a pole, tied the donkey's feet to it and raised the pole and the donkey to their shoulders

They went along amidst much laughter. Everyone they passed, pointed at them and laughed as if they might burst.

Eventually they came to a bridge that crossed a stream. The donkey just then managed to get one of its feet loose and kicked out, making the boy drop his end of the pole. In the struggle, the donkey fell over the bridge and because its forefeet were still tied together, would have drowned, had it not been for the farmer who dived into the river after it and managed to cut it free.

The farmer's wife was surprised when they arrived home early. Her husband and the donkey were drenched and cross, her son had a black eye where the donkey had kicked him and they had bought nothing at the market. When the farmer explained what had happened, his wife was furious. 'You should know by now never to listen to people who criticize you unless they do so constructively.'

'What does "constructively" mean?' asked the son.

'It means that next time we go to market we take your mother with us to carry our purchases, and leave the donkey at home,' said the father.

The Ugly Duckling

It was a glorious summer day in the country. The cornfields were golden and the hay stood neatly stacked in the meadow. A mother duck lay on her nest in a deserted spot near an old farm, waiting for her eggs to hatch. The time passed very slowly – especially since no one came to see her. At last, however, they began to crack open and, one by one, the little yellow chicks came blinking into the sunlight.

'Cheep, cheep,' they cried. 'How big the world is!'

'The world is far bigger than this,' said their mother. 'It stretches right across the canal and even beyond the next field, though I have never been there. Now, are you all here?' she continued. Then she noticed that one egg, the largest of all, lay still unopened in the nest. With a sigh, she resumed her seat, wondering to herself how much longer . . .

'Well, how's it going?' asked an old duck who had come to pay her a visit.

'This large egg just won't hatch. But look at the others. Aren't they the prettiest ducklings you ever saw?'

'Let me see the egg that won't hatch,' came the reply. 'Heavens! It looks like a turkey's egg. Don't waste your time on that one, dear. It will only bring you trouble and, believe me, it will never go near the water. Just teach the other children to swim and leave that one be. That's what I'd do.'

'Oh, one more day won't hurt me. I think I'll sit it out,' said the resolute mother.

'Well, you know best I'm sure,' said the old duck, shaking her head dubiously.

At last, the big egg burst open and out crept a very large, *very* ugly duckling.

The mother duck was worried. 'Can it really be a turkey chick?' she wondered. 'We'll find out for sure tomorrow.'

The next day she took all her chicks down to the water and jumped in. They all followed, one by one, *including* the ugly duckling.

'That's all right then. Now I know it isn't a turkey,' said the mother to herself.

She led the chicks into the farmyard to meet their relations, reminding them on the way to keep their toes turned out and look respectful.

But 'Oh no, not *more* newcomers,' was the cry, and one duck, catching sight of the poor little ugly duckling, flew into a disgusted rage, and bit it in the neck.

'It hasn't done you any harm!' cried its mother angrily.

'It's too big and odd-looking and ought to be taught a lesson,' said the rude duck.

'Such a shame. The *others* are so pretty,' remarked the old duck who had visited the nest the day before.

'This one may not be pretty, but it is very well-behaved and is the best swimmer of them all. I think he – for he is a drake – will grow up to be very strong. Beauty is not *so* important after all,' said the proud mother stoutly.

But the ugly duckling became the laughing stock of the yard. He was jeered at and pecked by the chickens as well as the ducks, while the turkey-cock, who was very full of himself, gobbled threateningly at him.

Over the next few days things went from bad to worse. The farmer's daughter kicked him as she fed the poultry and even his brothers and sisters turned against him and wished he would go away.

The ugly duckling was very miserable. Nobody wanted him on the farm, so he decided to go out onto the great moor where the wild ducks lived. The little birds in the bushes flew away when they saw him coming. 'That's because I am so ugly,' thought the duckling sadly, as he settled down alone among the reeds.

Later two wild geese flew by, making fun of the poor outcast as they passed. Suddenly, the duckling heard a loud 'Bang bang', and the two geese fell dead into the water. Hunters lay in wait all over the moor. The blue smoke of gunfire rose from the trees all around and the hunting dogs splashed noisily on every side. The ugly duckling was terrified.

As night fell, the din ceased. So, gathering his courage, the little duckling rose and fled through fields and meadows. A terrible storm raged and, after several hours, he was quite exhausted. He noticed a hut with a door hanging off its hinges. There was just enough space for him to slip inside. Here he found an old woman, a cat and a hen.

As soon as they saw the duckling the cat began to purr, the hen to cluck and the old woman, who had bad eyesight, to cry gleefully:

'What a stroke of luck! A great fat duck! Now we shall have fresh eggs every day. But – suppose it's a drake. Well, we must just wait and see.'

For three weeks she waited . . . but no eggs came . . .

One day the cat and the hen, who were accustomed to taking charge of the affairs of the household, questioned the duckling:

'Can you lay eggs?' demanded the hen haughtily.

'No', replied the bewildered duckling.

'Can you arch your back like this?' challenged the cat in a most alarming way.

'No, indeed,' said the poor duckling, almost beside himself with astonishment.

'Then kindly stay in your corner and hold your tongue,' snapped the two together.

Miserably, the ugly duckling obeyed. But when a breath of fresh air and a ray of sunshine crept through the door, he was seized with such a longing to swim on the water that he fled from the hut out into the wide world.

It was autumn and the leaves were turning brown and falling from the trees. One evening the ugly duckling saw a flock of lovely white birds with long necks flying above him. He turned round and round in the water to watch them, a strange feeling growing inside him. He admired their beauty and wished he were not so ugly himself.

The winter grew cold and harsh. The hole in which he swam became smaller and smaller as the ice grew thicker and thicker. Finally, worn out by his efforts to prevent it from freezing up altogether, he lay quite still, frozen fast into the ice.

Early next morning, a farmer saw him, broke the ice and took the duckling home to his children. They wanted to play with him, but the poor creature took fright, overturning first a milk churn and then a barrel of flour in his alarm. The farmer's wife screamed angrily at him and he flew away, wretched and exhausted . . .

Once again, the ugly duckling travelled long and far. He lay out on the moor, in a spot sheltered by the reeds, until one day the sun began to shine again and, at last, spring had arrived.

Now the ugly duckling noticed that his wings had grown bigger and stronger and that they would carry him easily as far as he wanted to go. One day he found himself in a beautiful sweet-smelling garden. Some elder trees bent their branches down to the water where three glorious swans were enjoying the sunshine. He recognized the magnificent birds and felt again the strange sadness. He flew towards them, crying humbly and piteously, 'Kill me – I am too ugly to share the world with you.'

All at once he caught sight of his reflection in the water. He stopped short, astonished. What trick was this? For there looking up at him was no hideous, clumsy-looking little bird but – he realized with joy – a *swan* as beautiful and graceful as the others.

The three great swans swam round him, stroking him welcomingly with their beaks and some children, coming into the garden, praised his youth and beauty and threw him some food.

Hiding his head under his wing, quite overcome by so much admiration, he thought to himself with a full heart, 'I never even *dreamed* of such happiness when I was just an ugly duckling!'

Rapunzel.

Once upon a time there lived a man and his wife who for many years had longed for a child. But their wish was not granted.

At the back of their house there was a little window that overlooked a beautiful garden, full of the finest flowers, fruit and vegetables that anyone could wish for. But no one ever ventured into the garden, for it belonged to one of the most wicked witches who ever lived.

One day the wife was looking out of the window into the garden when she noticed a bed full of the finest radishes she had ever seen. They were so fresh and pink and she wanted so much to eat some. As the days passed her desire for the radishes became so strong that she began to pine away. She grew pale and miserable.

'What is the matter, dear wife?' asked the man.

'I fear that I shall die if I do not have a few of the radishes that grow in the witch's garden,' she told him.

Now the man loved his wife so much that he decided that no matter what it cost, his wife would have some radishes.

He told his wife what he was going to do.

'Please be careful, If the witch catches you, she may punish you,' warned the woman.

'Don't worry about me,' replied the husband. 'I can take care of myself. His voice was calm and reassuring.

'At least wait until it is dark,' said the wife.

When night fell, he climbed the wall into the witch's garden, plucked a handful of radishes and took them back to his wife. As soon as she saw them she made a rich salad and ate and ate until she could eat no more.

She enjoyed them so much that the next day she longed for more. So once again at twilight, her husband crept into the garden and plucked a handful of radishes. Just as he was about to climb back over the wall, the witch suddenly appeared and pulled him down into the radish bed.

'How dare you steal my radishes? Thief! Villain!' she screamed. 'I have a mind to turn you into a radish as punishment.'

'Oh no, pleaded the man. 'Please I beg of you. Anything – everything I own, I will give to you, but please let me go.'

'Very well,' said the witch. 'But on one condition. You may have as many radishes as you like for your wife. But you will find that the child you have so long wished for, will soon come to you. When it is born, the child must be given to me. I will care for it.'

In his fear of the witch, the man promised to do as she said.

Sure enough a few months later, the wife was delivered of a beautiful baby girl. Almost as soon as the girl had been born, the witch appeared and took the child from the couple. 'I will call her Rapunzel and care for her well,' said the witch, as she left the cottage.

Rapunzel grew into the most beautiful child and when she was twelve years old, the witch locked her in a tower in the middle of a wood. The tower had no steps and no door, only a little window at the top. When the witch wished to be let in she would stand below and cry,

'Rapunzel, Rapunzel, let down your hair.'

Rapunzel had beautiful long hair that shone like gold. When she heard the voice of the witch she would undo the fastening on the window, unbind the ribbons in her hair and let it down. Her hair was so long that the tresses reached the ground, and the witch would climb up.

This went on for many years.

One day a king's son was riding by and he came upon the tower. As he drew near, he heard a voice singing so sweetly that he stopped and listened. It was Rapunzel who in her loneliness often tried to pass the time by singing sweet songs. The king's son wished to go to her, but he could find no door into the tower.

With a heavy heart he rode off. But Rapunzel's singing had so charmed him that every day he rode into the woods and listened.

One day, he was standing under a tree listening to Rapunzel's song when he saw the old witch approach. He heard her call out,

'Rapunzel, Rapunzel, let down your hair.'

Then he saw how Rapunzel let down her long tresses and watched the witch climb up to her.

The next day when it was growing dark, the king's son rode to the tower and cried,

'Rapunzel, Rapunzel, let down your hair.'

And she let down her hair and he climbed up.

Rapunzel was horrified when she saw who had climbed up her hair into her chamber, for she had never seen a man before. But the king's son was so kind and gentle. He told her how her song had charmed him and that he could have no peace until he had seen the owner of so beautiful a voice.

He was so kind that Rapunzel soon forgot her terror and when he asked her to marry him, she saw that he was young and handsome and she said to herself, 'I like him much more than my old witch.' Putting her hand into his she said, 'I would willingly go with you, but I cannot get out unless, each time you come, you bring a silken rope and I will make a ladder. When it is ready I will leave the tower, and we shall ride off together on your horse.'

They agreed that he should come in the evenings as the witch always came when it was light.

One day when the witch was with Rapunzel, she said unwittingly, 'Why is it that you climb up so slowly, when my love, the king's son is with me in moments?'

When the witch heard that someone had discovered the beautiful girl, she was furious. In her anger she seized Rapunzel by her hair and struck her several times. Then taking a pair of scissors from her pocket, she cut Rapunzel's long tresses from her head. She did not stop until all her beautiful golden hair lay on the floor of the chamber. Then with her evil magic, she sent Rapunzel to a barren wasteland where she hoped the king's son would never find her.

That evening the king's son rode up to the tower.

'Rapunzel, Rapunzel, let down your hair,' he cried.

The old witch in the chamber above let down the tresses that she had cut from Rapunzel's head. The king's son climbed up, but instead of his beloved Rapunzel, he was faced with the old witch, whose eyes were glittering with hatred. 'Ah!' she cried. 'You come for your love, but the sweet bird sits no longer in this nest. You will never see her again.'

With that, she pushed the king's son from the window ledge and he fell to the ground. As he fell, two thorns scratched his eyes and he was struck blind.

Day after day he stumbled through the forest, eating berries

Byeee!
I'm the
wicked Witch
fly me!
Eeeek!
Oh..what a wicked
witch!
It's a long
way down.

and roots, unable to see where he was going. His heart was full of grief for his lost love, but still he kept her song in his heart to remind him of his Rapunzel.

One day as he moved slowly through the forest he heard in the distance the very song that he had fallen in love with. He moved as quickly as he could, following the voice. Out of the forest he went and into the desert place where the witch had cast Rapunzel. Rapunzel looked up and saw her beloved stumbling towards her. She immediately ran towards him, took him in her arms and embraced him.

'My love, my love,' she cried. 'You have found me. The witch's spell is broken for ever. Only true blind love could defeat her. Your love must be the truest of all.'

When the king's son heard Rapunzel's voice and felt her in his arms, two tears fell from his eyes. Immediately his sight was restored to him and a smile spread across his face when he saw his beloved there in his arms.

The two made their way back to his father's kingdom, where they lived happily ever after.

A Sort of Cinderella.

'I never had this trouble with Cinderella. She went off to the ball, met her prince, married him and lived happily ever after. But you . . .'

Jennifer looked up at her fairy godmother. Unlike most fairy godmothers, she was wearing a raincoat and gumboots, and instead of a wand, she was carrying a rather battered umbrella. There was a cross expression on her face as she continued to complain to Jennifer.

'I never asked to be your fairy godmother, you know. It was pure bad luck that your name came out of the hat. You're not a bit like that nice Snow White girl. She was grateful. The presents she gave me must have been worth hundreds of pounds. Of course, she could afford it. The prince that I introduced her to was as rich as the queen of England.'

Jennifer sighed. 'I've told you. I don't believe in fairies. How many times do I have to tell you? I DO NOT BELIEVE IN FAIRIES.'

'Don't believe in fairies indeed! Look I'll prove it to you.'

The fairy godmother waved her umbrella twice around Jennifer and said some strange words. Suddenly Jennifer felt herself spinning round and round. There was the sound of strange music and stars seemed to flash past her eyes. When the spinning and the music and the flashing stopped, Jennifer found herself exactly where she had been before – sitting in her bedroom, with the strange woman who kept insisting she was her fairy godmother standing before her.

'Well!' said Jennifer. 'I told you, didn't I? Nothing happened, did it?'

'Ungrateful wretch,' shouted the fairy godmother. 'Didn't you feel yourself spinning? Didn't you hear music? Didn't you see stars flash before your eyes?'

'I felt a bit faint, that's all,' explained Jennifer. 'I expect it was the fish we had for supper.'

'Nonsense,' shrieked the fairy godmother, 'I'm just a bit out of practice, that's all. And it's all your fault. It's ten years since I took you over and because you say you don't believe in fairies, you have never asked me for anything. Not even a new dress, or new shoes. Nothing at all. What can I do to convince you, I wonder?'

The fairy godmother didn't say anything for a few minutes, but walked round and round Jennifer's bedroom.

'Do stop pacing around,' complained Jennifer. 'I'm trying to read, and it's very difficult with you here.'

The fairy godmother ignored Jennifer and carried on walking round the room. Suddenly she stopped. 'I know,' she said. 'I know exactly how to prove to you that I AM your fairy godmother. Here take my hand child. I'll show you.'

The old lady held out her hand, and Jennifer was very surprised to find herself reaching out to take it.

Once again, the fairy godmother waved her umbrella round her head and said some strange words. There was the same spinning

sensation and music and stars flashing, but this time when it all stopped, Jennifer and the fairy godmother were no longer in her bedroom at Number 21 Ferndale Road, but standing in the most beautiful room that Jennifer had ever seen. The walls were covered with hundreds of mirrors, each one richly decorated with gold. Between each mirror there were golden carvings, and the room was lit by thousands of candles that glowed from golden chandeliers. Jennifer was so surprised that she could not speak.

'Well child?' said the fairy godmother. 'You see! Only a fairy godmother could have brought you here.' There was a smug expression on her face as she spoke. 'This is where Cinderella lives now. Would you like to meet her?'

Jennifer was still too astonished to speak, so she nodded her head, her eyes wide open in amazement.

'Cooooeee!' called the fairy godmother. 'Cinderella! It's only me dear, your fairy godmother.'

A door at the other end of the room opened, and two uniformed footmen appeared. They bowed to the fairy godmother, who nodded back, the smug expression still on her face. Two of them stood at either side of the door. There was a rustling of silk and jingle of jewellery, and there stood Cinderella. She was very beautiful, just as Jennifer had imagined her when she was much younger and read fairy tales.

'You may come closer.' Cinderella's voice was as cold as ice. Jennifer clutched the fairy godmother's hand and the two of them approached the beautiful princess. The fairy godmother went right up to her and was about to kiss Cinderella on the cheek, when suddenly Cinderella held her hand out and signalled that the fairy godmother should curtsey before her. The magnificent rings on her fingers glistened in the golden candlelight.

'My subjects bow to me. Even the prince bows to me. I am the most beautiful woman in the land. Everyone bows to me.' The coldness of her voice froze Jennifer to the spot.

'Don't be impertinent to me, young woman,' said the fairy godmother. 'If it hadn't been for me you would still be in your step-mother's kitchen where I found you, peeling potatoes.'

'Nonsense,' cried Cinderella. 'I was determined to marry Charming long before you came on the scene. I'd known him for ages. His parents used to bring him to my father's house when they wanted to escape royal duties. If my own mother had not died and my father had not married that dreadful woman with her two ugly daughters, I would have married him long before I did.'

'It was I who got you to the ball, and dresses like the one you wore are not cheap, you know.' The fairy godmother was shaking with indignation as she spoke.

'What did you want me to do?' asked Cinderella. 'You said you were my fairy godmother and I *had* to get to the ball. Charming's mother was making such a fuss about him getting married, and I was afraid she would have forced him to choose someone else.'

'If you knew him all that time, why didn't he recognize you? Why did you leave at midnight? What about the glass slipper? How do you explain that?' roared the fairy godmother in a fury.

'How could he recognize me in that silly wig you made me put on? And as for leaving at midnight and dropping my slipper, I did that deliberately. How else would he have found me? I couldn't tell him I was Cinderella, not with my step-mother and step-sisters there. They would have dragged me away before he had a chance to ask me to marry him.'

'Why you scheming little vixen,' shouted the fairy godmother. 'All these spells! All that money! I've half a mind to magic you back to the kitchen where you belong.'

'Don't be silly,' said Cinderella. 'Charming would only come and get me. He adores me, I'm so beautiful. Now please go away. I find all this very tiresome.'

With that Cinderella turned on her heel and walked towards the door.

'I'll teach you a lesson,' cried the fairy godmother. She waved her umbrella four times in the air and muttered a spell. There was a great gust of wind and the door flew open. Cinderella began to spin and as she spun all her jewels fell from her fingers and from around her neck. The magnificent dress she had been wearing began to turn to rags. The silver slippers fell from her feet and the pearl combs slipped from her hair. When Cinderella stopped spinning she stood in the doorway, her hair tumbling in disarray around her shoulders. Smudges of soot were on her face, her dress was coarse and patched and her feet were bare.

'Oh please change her back,' pleaded Jennifer. 'She was so

beautiful. You can change her back and make her less proud. There must be a spell for that. You must. Please, Fairy Godmother.'

'What did you call me?'

'Fairy Godmother. I believe in you now,' said Jennifer. 'Please change her back again.'

'You really believe in me?' asked the fairy godmother.

'Yes. Oh yes.'

'Very well.' Once again the umbrella was waved in the air as the fairy godmother cast her spell. Cinderella spun round and her rags again became the beautiful dress she had been wearing. Jewels once again glistened on her fingers and around her neck. Jennifer was amazed to see that Cinderella was laughing happily. She was even more surprised when she saw the fairy godmother embrace her.

'It never fails, does it?' laughed Cinderella.

'No. How many is that?' chuckled the fairy godmother.

'I've lost count,' said Cinderella.

Jennifer ran up to them and asked what was happening.

'Well, you see,' said the fairy godmother, 'a long time ago all the magic went out of people's lives. I found that all my girls were just like you, and when I visited them to tell them I was their fairy godmother they never believed me. So Cinderella and I devised this little scheme. Everyone loves Cinderella, and when I bring children here to see her, we always pretend to have the same row. When I

magic her back to rags, all the children are so upset they plead with me to change her back to the Cinderella they love so much. And it convinces them that I am their fairy godmother. Now it's time we went back to Ferndale Road. I hope your parents haven't noticed you've gone. Parents get very upset about things like that.'

'Goodbye Jennifer,' smiled Cinderella.

The fairy godmother held Jennifer's hand and waved her umbrella in the air. Jennifer had just time to say goodbye to Cinderella before she felt herself spinning round and round. Music played in her ears and stars flashed past her eyes. In no time at all she was back in her bedroom.

There was no sign of her fairy godmother. Jennifer rubbed her eyes and thought to herself. 'I must have fallen asleep and dreamed it all. How strange!'

But she felt something in her hair. She went to the mirror and gasped when she saw that there was a beautiful pearl comb where her ribbon had been. It must have landed there when it flew out of Cinderella's hair.

She ran quickly over to the window and was just in time to see a strange little old lady wearing a raincoat and gumboots and carrying an umbrella, turn the corner out of Ferndale Road.

'Thank you Fairy Godmother,' she whispered. 'Thank you for bringing magic back into my life.'

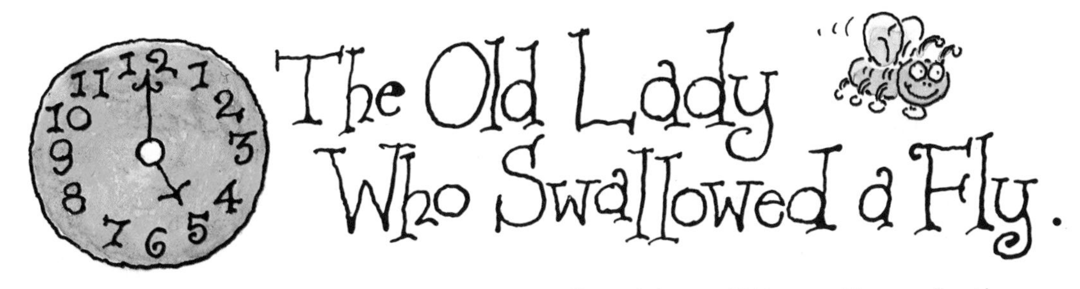

The Old Lady Who Swallowed a Fly.

There was once an old lady who lived in a little cottage in the country. The cottage was surrounded by a large garden, and the old lady was never happier than when she was working in it. She loved thinning out plants, weeding, growing flowers and vegetables, looking after her fruit trees and making sure that her garden was the best-kept in the district.

One day, when the sun was shining brightly, she was happily weeding the rose bed. Suddenly she sneezed. Her mouth flew open and she let out the loudest sneeze you ever heard. When she had recovered, she felt something wriggling and tickling and tickling inside her.

'Drat,' she said to herself. 'I must have swallowed a fly.'

She went into the cottage and poured herself a glass of water, hoping that when she drank it, the fly would drown. But it didn't. It just carried on wriggling and tickling and tickling inside her.

'I know,' she said. 'If I swallow a spider, that will kill the fly that's wriggling and tickling and tickling inside me.

So she went into the garden and found a plump spider. She closed her eyes and popped the spider into her mouth. She had to force herself to swallow it, because it was not very pleasant to feel the spider going down her throat, but the wriggling and tickling and tickling inside her was so annoying that she hoped that it would be worth it.

The wriggling and tickling became worse.

'Drat,' she said again. It was one of her favourite words and she used it whenever she was upset or annoyed. 'That spider may have swallowed the fly, but it's wriggling and tickling and tickling even more than the fly. How can I get rid of it?'

Just then, she noticed a blackbird fly down and pick up a spider in its orange beak. That gave her an idea.

'If I eat a bird, it will eat the spider that I ate to catch the fly that was wriggling and tickling and tickling inside me.'

Somehow the idea of eating a bird was not quite so bad as eating the spider. 'After all, I eat chicken and turkey, don't I?' she said to herself.

She went into the house and looked for the butterfly net that her son used to play with. She found it under the stairs with a lot of his old toys. When she looked at them all, her eyes misted with tears. It seemed like only yesterday that the house had been filled with her child's laughter, but he had long since grown up and left home. He was married now, and had children of his own. They came to visit occasionally, and sent her cards on her birthday and at Christmas, but she still missed her son.

She took the net into the garden and hid in the raspberry bushes. After a few minutes a little wren flew down. Quick as a flash, the old woman whipped the net over it, and before she could think about it, she grabbed the poor bird from the net and swallowed it.

The wriggling and tickling and tickling inside her became worse almost immediately. She said something much worse than 'drat', so much worse that the vicar who was cycling past the garden was so shocked that he fell off his bicycle.

Now the old lady was a very determined old lady. The more the wriggling and tickling and tickling inside her went on, the more determined she was to get rid of it.

'What eats birds?' she asked herself. She looked up and just at that moment saw her old cat creeping through the cabbage patch, tracking a bird. 'Here, Kitty,' she called out, and the old cat, expecting a nice titbit, immediately forgot the bird and went running to her mistress. Imagine her surprise when instead of getting a juicy piece of fish, the old lady picked her up and swallowed her whole.

'That will get rid of the bird I swallowed to get rid of the spider I swallowed to get rid of the fly I swallowed that wriggled and tickled

and tickled inside me,' the old lady said to herself smugly. But the wriggling and tickling and tickling became worse and worse.

This time she said a word that, had the vicar heard it, he would have fallen off his bicycle and never got up again.

The old lady was by this time so full that she could hardly move. 'I must get rid of the cat I swallowed to get rid of the bird I swallowed to get rid of the spider I swallowed to get rid of the fly I swallowed that wriggled and tickled and tickled inside me', she said to herself.

She was wondering what to do, when her dog ran up to her and began to lick her. 'There is nothing else for it,' she sighed and popped her poor dog into her mouth.

Now I don't know if you know anyone who has ever eaten a fly, a spider, a bird, a cat and a dog, but I am sure that you can imagine how uncomfortable it must be. The old lady lay on the ground groaning, unable to move. There was one enormous wriggling and tickling and tickling inside her. She moaned and moaned and moaned, making a sound a bit like a bleating goat. In fact, it was so like a goat bleating, that the old nanny goat in the field next to her garden heard it and thought it was her sister. The old nanny goat was very lonely. She had not seen her sister for a long time, and she thought how nice it would be to have a good gossip with her. So she found a gap in the old lady's hedge and squeezed through it. Imagine her surprise when she found the old lady lying on the ground looking three times as big as she usually did. She was rolling around, clutching her stomach,mumbling something about a dratted fly that had been wriggling and tickling and tickling inside her. The goat went up to her to see if there was something she could do to help the old lady.

Can you think what happened next? You are not going to believe it, but the old lady took one look at the nanny goat, grabbed it by the neck and swallowed it. I suppose she thought that the goat would get rid of the dog she had swallowed to get rid of the cat she had swallowed to get rid of the bird she had swallowed to get rid of the spider she had swallowed to get rid of the fly that had been wriggling and tickling and tickling inside her.

The old lady tried to get up. But she could not.

'I can't stay here all night,' she said. So she rolled over and over, trying to get to her cottage. Unfortunately she found herself rolling away from the cottage, down the garden path, through the gate, down the lane and into the field where her neighbour kept his horse. When she saw the horse her eyes lit up. 'The horse is bound to catch the goat that I swallowed to catch the dog I swallowed to catch the cat I swallowed to catch the bird that I swallowed to catch the spider that I swallowed to catch the fly that I swallowed that wriggled and tickled and tickled inside me.'

The horse knew the old lady. She often gave it lumps of sugar, so it went across to where she lay hoping for something sweet to nibble. It lowered its head . . . and yes . . . you're right . . . the old lady opened her mouth wide and swallowed the poor old horse.

Now you may expect that anyone who had swallowed a horse, a goat, a dog, a cat, a bird, a spider and a fly all in one day would die. But fortunately for her, just as she swallowed the horse the vicar cycled past. When he heard the commotion he stopped his bicycle and ran into the field. He saw the old lady lying there with a horse's tail coming out of her mouth, so he rushed over to her and pulled and pulled on the tail.

With a huge 'plop' the bewildered looking horse popped out of the old lady's stomach. The vicar saw that there was a tail hanging from the horse's mouth so he pulled and pulled on it, and with a loud bleat, the goat came out of the horse's mouth. No sooner had it come out than it sneezed. With a great rush of air the dog flew out of the goat's mouth and from the dog's mouth came the cat, and from the cat's mouth flew the bird and from the bird's mouth flew the spider and from the spider's mouth flew the fly.

'Bless you vicar,' cried the old lady, 'I thought it was all over with me.'

Just then the vicar sneezed loudly, and as he did so a very strange expression came over his face.

'What's wrong?' asked the old lady.

'I think I've swallowed a fly,' said the vicar.

'Don't worry,' the old lady said consolingly. 'I know just what to do . . .'

The King's Enormous Feet.

Many centuries ago there lived a king who had the most enormous feet you could ever wish to see. They were so huge that no shoes could ever be found to fit them.

The royal shoemaker could never find enough leather to make even one shoe, let alone a pair, and the royal sockmaker could never find enough wool to cover the king's toes, let alone the whole of his feet.

The king began to get more and more tired of walking around the palace in his bare feet. So one day he ordered the royal letter-writer to come to his chambers with pen and ink. The king wanted to draw up a proclamation which was to be pinned up in the town square for all his subjects to see.

The proclamation was duly dictated and nailed up on the proclamation board:

BY ROYAL COMMAND, it read, THE PERSON WHO CAN SOLVE THE PROBLEM OF THE KING'S FEET WILL BE REWARDED WITH ONE HUNDRED PIECES OF GOLD.

'One hundred pieces of gold,' murmured one citizen. 'That's fifty per foot. Not bad. Not bad at all.'

People from all over the land flocked to the square. They stood around in small groups discussing the king's enormous feet. None of them had any idea what to do about them. None, that is, apart from a poor boat-maker. He read the proclamation and hurried back to his boat yard. He locked the doors and set to work. For days, no one saw the boat-maker, but they knew that he was inside for they could hear him sawing and chopping and banging and planing. None of his friends could understand what was going on behind the locked doors.

Seven days later the boat-maker came out pulling behind him a large box on wheels. It was such a heavy box that the boat-maker's three sons were helping to pull it. No one could see inside the box, for the top of it was above eye level.

The boat-maker and his sons pulled the box through the streets to the palace gates, up the palace steps and into the throne room. The king was seated on the throne, his enormous feet sticking out in front of him.

'Sire,' began the boat-maker, 'I have made you a fine pair of shoes.'

The king had heard this before, and said, 'Oh really,' in a most bored voice. 'I expect that they will be much too small like all the others.'

But he slowly rose from the throne and lifted the lid of the box.

He beckoned to a royal page and ordered him to take the shoes out of the box. The page obeyed immediately, and when he had taken them out, all the courtiers gasped in astonishment, for there was a pair of WOODEN shoes.

The wooden shoes were a perfect fit and the king was so delighted with them that he clumped up and down the throne room in them, showing them off to the whole court. Everyone was so happy to see the king pleased at last that they cheered and cheered.

The king beamed with pleasure and told the boat-maker to come closer. 'These shoes fit so perfectly I shall not need to wear any socks with them. What do you call them?'

Now the boat-maker had no idea what to call the wooden shoes, so he said to the king, 'I made them out of some . . .' Here he meant to say 'conifer logs', but he was so nervous at being spoken to by the king that he ran the two words together, and somehow they came out as one word – *clogs*. And that is what they have been called ever since.

The Princess and The Pea.

The kingdom of Crystal was a very beautiful land and was ruled over with great fairness by King Simon and his wife Queen Aurora. They had one son, who was as handsome as princes in storybooks are meant to be. The royal family were greatly loved by their subjects and they loved their people in return.

As the prince, who was called Guy, grew up he became even more handsome and many of the ladies at court fell in love with him, but he was more interested in his horse and hunting and shooting and fishing with his friends than he was in girls.

Just before his twentieth birthday, the king and queen told him that the time had come for him to be married, and that if he did not want to choose his own bride, then one would be found for him. Guy shrugged his shoulders indifferently and called for his horse to be brought to him so that he could go hunting.

And so a proclamation was issued to all the neighbouring kingdoms telling their rulers that a bride was to be chosen for Guy and that she must be a lady of royal blood.

When the proclamation reached everyone, the neighbouring princesses refused to go and be considered as a bride for Guy. They had all heard how he was more interested in horses and in hunting than in girls.

'But we must send someone,' said King John to his wife, Queen Mary. 'King Simon and Queen Aurora will take great offence if we do not send our daughter Princess Lise.' But the princess refused to go. 'Send Duke Wilfred's daughter, instead,' she said. 'No one in Crystal has ever seen me, so they won't know the difference.'

'It's no good, she won't go,' said Queen Eva to her husband King Peter.

'But we must send someone,' said the king. 'It's only polite.'

'Very well,' said the queen. 'We'll send the Countess Elisabetta. After all, no one in Crystal has ever seen the princess, so they won't know the difference.'

'I am not going,' cried Princess Lucia, daughter of King Eric and Queen Patricia. 'I've heard all about him and his hunting. Send the Lady Violet instead. After all no one in Crystal has ever seen me, so they won't know, will they?'

'But why can't I go?' asked Princess Mary of Rotania. 'It's not fair. You never let me go anywhere,' she complained to her mother, Queen Antonia, wife of King Gustav.

'Someone's got to stay here and look after us,' said the queen. 'We allowed your sisters to marry foreign princes and never saw them again afterwards. If you are going to marry, you must marry one of the courtiers here, in Rotania.'

'I think you are a . . . a . . . a . . . silly old lady,' shouted Mary, and ran from the throne room.

A few weeks later a great ball was held in the golden room at the palace of King Simon and Queen Aurora. All the ladies and gentlemen of the court were dressed in their finest silks and velvets. The musicians played waltzes and polkas and mazurkas, and as the dancers moved in time to the music, their fine clothes floated around them in a dazzling array of colours. At one end of the room sat the king and queen; Prince Guy was seated on a footstool just in front of them, looking very bored.

Suddenly the doors at the end of the room flew open, and there stood Duke Wilfred's daughter looking just like the Princess Lise whom she was pretending to be. Beside her was Countess Elisabetta, looking every inch the daughter of King Peter and Queen Eva, whom she was pretending to be. And beside her stood the Lady Violet, looking just as beautiful as Princess Lucia, whom she was pretending to be.

They had all arrived earlier that day and spent hours dressing and making themselves look pretty.

The three 'princesses' walked slowly up to the throne and curtseyed deeply before the king and queen. When they saw Prince Guy their hearts almost stopped beating, he was so handsome.

'Welcome my dears,' said the queen. 'I hope that you are not too tired after your long journeys.'

'Oh no, ma'am,' they all cried together. 'We can't wait to dance with the prince.'

'Very well,' said the queen. 'Guy! Dance!'

'Must I? You know how much I hate all this nonsense,' said Guy.

'YES, YOU MUST,' said the queen, in a very frosty voice.

'Oh very well. You!' He pointed at the daughter of Duke Wilfred and led her onto the dance floor.

A few minutes later he was dancing with Countess Elisabetta, and a few minutes after that with the Lady Violet. He was not at all impressed with any of the 'princesses', found their chatter tiresome and he hated dancing anyway.

As soon as he had finished his third dance, he left the ballroom saying that he had a headache.

'Children!' said Aurora to Simon as their son disappeared. 'Why do we bother? He must choose a bride soon.'

'They all look very well to me,' said the king smiling at Duke Wilfred's daughter as he spoke, thinking her to be the daughter of the king and queen of Nureyvia.

'Now my dears,' said the queen to the three 'princesses'. 'Off to bed with you all.'

The three girls curtseyed and did as they were told.

The next morning the king and queen were breakfasting with Prince Guy, who was looking very sullen. It was a beautiful morning and he would much rather have been out hunting than wasting time eating breakfast.

The queen was having her second cup of tea when the three 'princesses' came down.

'Well my dears!' she smiled at them. 'How did you sleep?'

'Beautifully,' replied the Duke Wilfred's daughter. 'My bed had ten feather mattresses on it. I have never slept so well.'

'Gloriously,' replied the Countess Elisabetta. 'I too had ten feather mattresses on my bed. I slept so deeply, I did not want to leave my bed this morning.'

'Marvellously,' said the Lady Violet. 'I have never slept on feather mattresses before. It was blissful.'

'Princesses!' roared the queen. 'Call yourselves princesses? Why you're all impostors – all three of you! Get out of my sight and leave this kingdom for ever.'

The three 'princesses' turned and ran as quickly as they could from the parlour. Within minutes they had packed their bags and left the palace.

'Thank goodness that's all over,' said Guy, rising from the table. 'May I go hunting now?'

'It's all your fault,' shouted the furious queen. 'If you were a bit less interested in hunting and more interested in getting married, this would never have happened.'

'But what has happened?' asked the king who had been quite bemused by the queen's explosion of anger and had been very sorry for the three girls, especially Duke Wilfred's daughter, whom he had taken to be the Princess Lise of Nureyvia.

'Don't you see,' cried the queen. 'None of them sent their daughters. They were all imposters. Oh, the embarrassment of it! How can I hold my head up again?' And having said that, she ran from the room, almost tripping over one of the many Pekinese that were forever snapping around her ankles.

'I must say, Guy,' said the king, 'there are times when I quite understand that you would rather hunt than get married. Now I'll have to go and calm her down. If I were you I would make myself scarce for the rest of the day.'

So Prince Guy went down to the stables and ordered his horse to be saddled.

A few minutes later he was as happy as he was handsome, riding through the woods in pursuit of a wild boar. Suddenly his horse reared up and he fell from the saddle. He got to his feet and went to see what had made his horse throw him.

Lying in the pathway was the most beautiful girl Guy had ever seen. She was obviously a servant girl, judging from her clothes. Her hair was the colour of pure gold and her skin was as soft as velvet. Her mouth was a perfect bow shape and her fingers were long and fine. He knelt down beside her and raised her head in his arms. As she moved, she moaned slightly and her eyes fluttered

open. They were as blue as fresh cornflowers. He immediately forgot about the boar. All he could think of was the beautiful girl he held in his arms.

Very gently he lifted her and put her on his horse's back. Taking the reins in his hand he led her back to the palace.

The king and queen saw him coming and ran out to the courtyard to find out what had happened.

'Who is she?' asked the queen.

'How did you find her?' asked the king.

As the prince was explaining, the girl suddenly realized where she was. She was most embarrassed and tried to curtsey to the king and queen. When she looked up at Guy, she blushed slightly and Guy fell more deeply in love with her, for her blush made her even more beautiful than before.

'What happened my child?' asked the queen.

'I was out riding and my horse must have thrown me,' she said.

It's no good I can't sleep!
It feels as if theres a pea in the bed.
Would you like to borrow my teddy?
'ello princess.

'Do you like riding?' asked Guy.

'More than anything else in the world,' said the girl.

'Do not say another word,' said the king. 'You are much too tired to explain any more.' He turned and called for a servant to take the girl to a bedroom to rest. 'Take her to the room that one of the impostors slept in last night.'

'But Sire,' began the servant, 'the mattresses are still on the beds.'

'No matter,' said the king. 'Do as I say.'

'Why Guy!' said the queen, when the girl had gone. 'There's a very odd expression on your face.'

The poor prince blushed as deeply as the girl had. 'It's that girl. I love her so. I want to marry her.'

'You can't marry her,' said the queen. 'You are a prince. You must marry someone of royal blood. And you can see from her clothes that she is hardly that.'

Poor Guy. For the first time in his life he was in love and could not marry the girl of his choice. No matter how hard he tried to explain to his parents, they insisted that he had to marry a princess. All day the battle raged. Guy insisted that if he could not marry her, he would marry no one else. The king and queen insisted that he must marry, but not her. His bride had to be a princess. The row carried on through dinner and Guy was saying for the hundredth time that if he could not marry her, he would not marry at all, when suddenly the girl who was the cause of it all appeared.

'Did you sleep well, my dear?' asked the queen, more out of politeness than interest.

'No. I have never been so miserable in my life. The bed looked so comfortable with all these mattresses, but it turned out to be horrid. A few minutes ago I could stand it no longer and I decided to see if there was something under the mattresses. Look!' She held out something in her hand as she spoke. 'Some cruel person put

this under the bottom-most mattress. How can anyone be expected to sleep on top of that?'

In her hand she was holding a tiny pea.

'But only a princess could have failed to sleep in that bed because of the pea,' said the queen. 'That's why I put it there.'

'You put it there?' said the king. 'But why?'

'Because I suspected as soon as I set eyes on these three girls that they were not real princesses. Something told me. I don't know what, but a mother always knows, you know.'

'Are you indeed a princess?' asked Guy.

'Yes. I am the Princess Mary of Rotania. We were sent the proclamation, but my parents wouldn't let me come. I decided to slip away and come despite them, but I had to borrow my maid's clothes so that I would not be recognized. That's why I'm dressed like this.'

'Then will you marry me?' asked Guy, dropping to his knees.

'Only if you promise to take me hunting with you every day. I love hunting, but my parents say it is not ladylike, so they forbid me to do it. I slip away occasionally but it's very difficult. My parents are so possessive, they always want to know where I am and what I'm doing. It's no fun being a princess in Rotania, I can tell you.'

'Well I hope that you'll enjoy being a princess in this land my dear,' said the king, smiling at her as he spoke. 'Come, let us leave them alone,' he said to the queen.

And the king and queen left Guy and Mary together. And they have been together ever since.

Soldier, Soldier, Will You Marry Me?

Once upon a time there was a beautiful young girl who lived in a small town where very little happened. As she grew older she became even more beautiful and many young men fell in love with her. They all asked her to marry them, but the young girl was very proud as well as very beautiful and she thought that she was far too good for any of them.

One day a battalion of soldiers arrived in the town. They looked splendid in their scarlet jackets and white breeches, and their black boots were so highly polished that they gleamed in the spring sunshine. There was one young officer who was as handsome as the girl was beautiful. His hair was dark and curly and his eyes were of the deepest shade of green that the girl had ever seen. He was taller than all the other soldiers, and when he smiled she could see that he had shining white teeth. When he gave orders to his men, she could hear that his voice was deep and musical. For the first time in her life, the girl fell in love and became determined to marry the handsome soldier.

Because nothing much happened in the town, many of the families gave parties for the officers. Their conversation was bright and witty and came as a welcome change from the usual chatter about crops and weather and the price of food. The young girl was invited to many of these gatherings and often talked with the young officer. After several meetings she began to think he liked her as much as she liked him.

After a few months when the two had met each other many times, she asked him to go on a picnic with her.

The day was bright and sunny and her heart was full of happiness as she prepared the food. She packed a wicker hamper with all sorts of lovely cold meat, salad and a lots of fruit. She put some sweet wine into the hamper and when she and her officer arrived at the chosen spot, the soldier tied string round the necks of the bottles and lowered them into the stream so that the wine would stay cool.

They talked of this and that and the girl felt herself fall more and more in love with him as the day passed.

Eventually she could bear it no longer and cried, 'Oh soldier, I love you so much, will you marry me?' The soldier who had been lying down basking in the glorious sunshine, sat upright and said:

'I cannot. There is a law that says that officers are not allowed to get married in their uniforms and I have no coat to wear.'

The girl suddenly remembered that in the attic of her house, her grandmother's chest had stood unopened for many years, and she dimly recalled that there had been a coat in it. She ran home and went up to the attic. She opened the chest and there, on the top, was a fine yellow coat with black trimmings. She took it out and ran back to the picnic spot where she gave it to the soldier and said, 'Here, put on this coat.'

The soldier did so, and very handsome he looked.

'Oh soldier, soldier will you marry me?' she asked him.

'I fear I cannot, for I have no hat to put on,' he said.

So once again she ran back to the attic and opened the chest. There was a beautiful hat in it, made of the same yellow material as the coat, and a magnificent feather adorned its brim.

She hurried back to the soldier who was still wearing the yellow coat.

'Here,' she said. 'Put on this hat.'

The soldier did so and looked as handsome as handsome could be in his fine yellow coat and matching hat with the feather.

'Oh soldier, soldier, will you marry me?' she asked for the third time.

'I cannot,' he said, 'for I have no breeches to put on,' said the soldier.

'Breeches,' she thought to herself. 'I'm sure I saw a pair in grandmother's chest.' So she ran back to the attic, and sure enough there was a fine pair of breeches made of soft green silk. She took them back to her soldier as fast as she could and told him to put them on.

The soldier went behind some bushes to change his breeches and when he stepped out she had never seen anyone look as handsome as he did. The green silk of the breeches was exactly the same colour as his eyes, and showed off the yellow coat and hat perfectly.

'Now, please will you marry me?' she asked.

'I fear I cannot, for I have no boots to put on,' the soldier replied.

'I swear that if I did not love him so much, I would feel that he was mocking me,' the girl thought. But stifling this doubt she ran back to the attic and found a superb pair of leather boots in the chest. She hurried back to her soldier and held them out to him. 'Boots,' she said. 'You need boots. Here are boots.'

The soldier put on the black boots and when she looked at him all her doubts vanished into thin air. He was without doubt the handsomest man in the world in the yellow coat, feathered hat, green breeches and black boots.

'Oh, soldier, soldier will you marry me?' she asked him again.

'I fear I cannot, for I have no gloves to put on,' the soldier said.

'A coat. A hat. Breeches. Boots. Now gloves.' The sweet expression on the girl's face did not alter. 'I think I saw a pair of gloves in grandmother's chest when I went back to get the boots. I shall fetch them for you. While I'm there is there anything else you need? The day is so fine it is such a shame to spend so much of it indoors,' the girl said.

'I don't think so,' said the soldier. 'Unless there's a shirt, for this one is badly in need of mending and perhaps some lace cuffs and a lace jabot. And my coat and breeches are so fine that they show up the poor quality of my belt.'

'Don't worry,' said the girl. 'I shall see if there is anything left in he chest.'

She made her way back to the house and paused in the kitchen to look for a bag. When she found one she went up to the attic. The chest was almost empty by this time, but sure enough there were a pair of soft white leather gloves, lace cuffs and jabot and a leather belt with a magnificent gold buckle. She put them all in the bag and closed the now empty chest.

She made her way back to her soldier and gave him the bag. The soldier buckled the belt around his waist. He attached the lace cuffs to his sleeves and tied the lace jabot round his neck. He pulled on the leather gloves.

He was without doubt not only the handsomest of men, but also the best dressed one that the girl had ever seen. And as he stood in the late afternoon sunshine, the girl knew that this time when she asked him to marry her, there could be no excuse for his not accepting.

'Oh soldier, soldier will you marry me?' she sighed.

'Er . . . er . . .' he stammered.

'Please!' She persisted.

'It's . . . er . . . it's . . .'

'WILL YOU MARRY ME?'

'I . . . f . . . f . . . f . . .'

'WELL!'

'I fear that I cannot,' he said, 'for I have a wife already.'

And with that he bowed to the girl, picked up his uniform which was lying nearby and left her.

He never saw her again, but the next morning a large chest was delivered to him at his barracks!

The Honest Woodcutter.

Have you ever noticed that the heroes of old stories are often woodcutters? Perhaps long ago there were many more woodcutters than there are today. This story is all about one of these woodcutters who lived in a far-away land many hundreds of years ago, long before you or even your parents were born. Like most woodcutters, he was very poor, and no matter how hard he worked he never had enough money. Also, like most woodcutters, he had a wife who loved him dearly and a few sheep.

One day, the woodcutter was out in the forest cutting wood, which is after all what woodcutters do for a living, when he heard someone crying for help.

The woodcutter ran through the woods to the place where the voice seemed to be coming from and looked all around him. But he could see no one. He looked up into the trees, but still could see no one. Suddenly he realized that the voice was coming from beneath the ground.

'Help! Help!' the voice cried.

The woodcutter walked slowly forward. Next moment he had almost fallen into a deep pit.

'Is there anyone there?' the woodcutter shouted down into the pit.

'Of course there is,' yelled the voice angrily. 'It is I. Lord Crullus Mostus the emperor's lord chamberlain.'

(Have you ever noticed how so many nasty people seem to have suitable names?)

When the woodcutter heard the voice tell him his name he was afraid, for the lord chamberlain was known to be a cruel tyrant.

'Oh Lord Crullus Mostus, what are you doing in this pit?' he asked.

'Dolt!' shouted Lord Crullus Mostus. 'I had this pit dug to catch the wild animals that roam in the forest.'

Now the woodcutter did not like being called a dolt, but he knew that he had to help Lord Crullus Mostus out of the pit.

'Don't just stand there,' cried Crullus Mostus. 'Get a rope and help me out. There is a monkey and a lion and a snake in the pit and I am sure they will soon attack me.'

'I will have to go into town and buy one, for I am a poor peasant and do not possess a rope,' the woodcutter replied. 'It's a long way to go and it will be almost dark before I return, so I will not be able to cut any wood to sell to pay my rent.'

'Fool! I will repay you handsomely,' cried Lord Crullus Mostus.

So the woodcutter ran as fast as he could into town and bought a length of rope with his last few pence. Just as it was getting dark, he was back at the pit.

'I will throw the rope down. Catch it and I will pull you up,' said the woodcutter.

'Hurry, peasant,' Lord Crullus Mostus wailed. 'I fear that the lion is about to attack me. And the monkey that fell into the pit with the lion is about to attack me. And the snake that fell into the pit is about to bite me. They are all looking at me very fiercely. So hurry up.'

The woodcutter tied one end of the rope round a nearby tree and threw the other end down into the pit. But before the tyrant Lord Crullus Mostus could touch it, the lion grasped the rope and clambered up. When it reached firm ground, the lion bowed to the woodcutter and growled its thanks to him. Down below, Crullus Mostus again tried to get hold of the rope, but the monkey shook it from his hand and quickly climbed out of the pit. Like the lion, it bowed to the woodcutter before it ran off into the forest. Again, Crullus Mostus tried to get to the rope, but before he could take it in his hands, the snake coiled round it and slithered up and out of the pit. When it saw the woodcutter, it stood on its tail and bowed its thanks. The astonished woodcutter was too surprised to say a word.

A few minutes later, a very hot and bothered Lord Crullus Mostus managed to climb up the rope and was out of the pit.

'Idiot!' he shouted at the woodcutter, knocking him to the ground. And with that he strode off into the forest.

'But master,' cried the poor woodcutter, trying to rise to his feet, 'you promised to reward me.'

'Stuff and nonsense,' retorted the wicked lord over his shoulder. 'You shall receive no reward from me.'

A few days later, the poor woodcutter was at work as usual in the forest when he saw ten donkeys coming towards him, each one laden with a heavy pack. Behind the donkeys, the woodcutter saw the lion he had rescued from the pit. The lion indicated with its paw that the donkeys and all their packs now belonged to the woodcutter. Then it bowed and made its way back into the forest. The astonished woodcutter led the donkeys home where he and his wife were amazed to find that the packs were filled to the top with gold.

'We are rich, wife,' the woodcutter cried in delight. 'Now I need no longer cut wood for a living.' 'You didn't make much of a living out of cutting wood when you had to,' said his wife.

But the next morning his wife said to him. 'I don't want you here under my feet all day. I have work to do. Go into the forest and cut some wood for our fire.'

The woodcutter did as he was told, but forgot to take his axe with him. He was just about to go back to the cottage to collect it, when the monkey he had rescued from the pit appeared. It immediately began to break off little twigs and branches from the trees, and by the end of the day there was a huge pile of firewood

ready to be taken home. The monkey helped the woodcutter to carry it and when they had finished the task the monkey bowed and made its way back into the forest.

The following morning the woodcutter was sitting in a chair in his little patch of garden when the snake he had rescued from the pit appeared. It slithered up close to the woodcutter and dropped a magnificent jewel at his feet. It glittered in the morning sunshine and dazzled the woodcutter with its glowing colours. The snake reared up and bowed to the woodcutter, then slithered off into the forest.

The woodcutter ran into town with the jewel and took it to a man who knew all about precious stones. When he saw it the man's eyes lit up as brightly as the jewel. 'I will give you any sum you want for this,' he said to the woodcutter. But the woodcutter refused to sell and went home.

News of the woodcutter's fabulous stone soon spread far and near, and came at last to the ears of the emperor. He summoned the woodcutter to appear before him with the stone.

When the emperor saw it, he said to the woodcutter, 'I will give you anything you want for that stone, for I must have it. And if you do not sell it to me you must leave my land forever.' The poor woodcutter had no choice but to sell the precious stone to the emperor. But the emperor was a fair man, and gave him five sacks of gold and five sacks of silver for it which the woodcutter did not need as he was quite rich now.

As the woodcutter was about to leave, the emperor called him back and asked how a poor woodcutter had come to own such a magnificent jewel.

The woodcutter explained about helping the lion, the monkey and the snake out of the pit, as well as Lord Crullus Mostus, the lord chamberlain.

'And how did my chamberlain, Crullus Mostus, reward you?' demanded the king.

'He called me an idiot and knocked me to the ground,' replied the woodcutter, not out of spite, but because he was an honest man and always told the truth.

When he heard this, the emperor was furious and summoned Lord Crullus Mostus to come before him. The guards left the throne room and went to search for the unsuspecting chamberlain.

When Lord Crullus Mostus saw the emperor in a rage he was

afraid, and when he saw the woodcutter with him, he began to tremble with terror.

'Is what this man told me true?' roared the emperor.

'Y..Y..Y..our ..m..majesty,' stammered the chamberlain, 'I ...'

But before he could go on the emperor called for silence. 'I can see that it is true. You are not fit to live,' he said. 'Guards, take him away and have him executed.'

'Oh no, your majesty,' cried the woodcutter, falling to his knees. 'Pray do not kill him.'

The emperor was so moved by the woodcutter's appeal that he changed his mind, and instead of having the chamberlain killed, he ordered that all his lands and wealth be taken from him and given to the woodcutter. He also banished him from the country for ever.

The emperor made the woodcutter his chief gamekeeper and gave him a fine house on the fringes of the forest where he and his wife lived happily ever after.

The Wedding Shirt.

There was once a king who had three sons and one daughter. The three young men were brave and daring, and the king was extremely proud of them, especially as their fame had spread far beyond the boundaries of his kingdom. His daughter was called Ileana and she was as beautiful as her brothers were brave. She was so beautiful that kings and princes from all over the world came to the royal palace to try to win her hand in marriage. But the princess fell in love with only one of them. He was the son of a neighbouring king and his name was Valiant.

When the princess told her father that she wanted to marry Valiant, he was very happy and embraced the young man. He sent messengers to every corner of the realm to announce that his beloved daughter Ileana was to be married to Prince Valiant.

Within a few days, however, the messengers arrived with sad news. They had discovered that across the borders of the kingdom, the king's enemies had gathered and were about to invade the land. And so, instead of preparing for his daughter's wedding, the old king sadly began to prepare for war. He summoned his three sons and told them to muster their troops. Valiant immediately volunteered to ride alongside them, and so a few days after the messengers had returned, Ileana sadly watched as her father, her brothers and her lover rode out at the head of their army.

Each day Ileana sat in her chamber waiting for news of her loved ones. To pass the time she began to embroider a wedding shirt for Valiant to wear on their wedding day.

Days turned into weeks and no news came. Ileana began to be afraid, so she released the little magic bird that she kept in a golden cage in her bedroom. This magical bird could speak the language of humans.

'Fly little bird,' said Ileana, as she held it in her hands. 'Fly and bring me news of my loved ones.'

So the little bird spread its wings and flew out of the window, over mountains and across valleys and lakes on and on till it reached the battlefields.

Ileana sat and waited. In the early hours of the morning a few days later she was awakened from her sleep by the sound of the little magic bird tapping on her window.

When Ileana asked it for news, it replied, 'I have flown over the battlefields and seen your three brothers fighting as bravely as lions.'

When she heard this, Ileana wept tears of happiness and a few of the tears landed on the wedding shirt that she was embroidering for Valiant. Where each tear fell, a silver moonbeam was magically sewn into the shirt.

Then the bird spoke again. 'But as I was flying home, I saw your father, lying dead on the battlefield.'

When she heard this, Ileana wept tears of sadness and a few of the tears dropped on the wedding shirt. Where each tear fell, a star was magically sewn into the shirt.

The next morning Ileana sent the bird out once more. While she waited she picked up her embroidery and patiently sewed all day until the magic bird returned.

That evening the bird returned and tapped on the window. Ileana ran and unfastened the catch to let the little bird in. 'Your Highness,' it said, 'as I flew over the battlefield I saw all the king's sons lying dead on the battlefield.'

Ileana's tears of sadness fell onto the wedding shirt, and where each tear fell a butterfly was magically sewn into it. She thought that she could bear no more grief, but the little bird continued. 'Your Highness, as I flew home, I saw Valiant fighting bravely against many of the enemy. He fought as valiantly as his name, but the odds were too great and he was killed as I watched.'

On hearing this, poor Ileana wept tears of bitterness which fell on the wedding shirt. And where each tear fell a little blue flower, as blue as her eyes, was embroidered on the wedding shirt. All that was left to remind her of her father, her brothers and her lover were the stars, the butterflies and the little blue flowers, magically embroidered on the wedding shirt.

Ileana knew that the enemy, having won the war, would soon march on the palace. She ordered that it should be burned to the ground so that when the conquerors arrived there would be nothing for them to capture but smouldering ashes.

Ileana fled into the woods taking only the wedding shirt with her. She thought sorrowfully of her father, her brothers and her lover, Valiant and as she did so she unfolded the wedding shirt and waved it in the gentle breeze. And the wind gathered up the stars from the shirt and sprinkled them around the heavens. It gathered up the butterflies and they flew off in all directions. It caressed the shirt with its soft breath and the little flowers were scattered over the grass.

And that is why, today, stars shine in the heavens, butterflies drift over meadows on summer days and the grass is dotted with violets as blue as Ileana's eyes.

Ileana's love for her father, her brothers and her prince has never died – for true love never does.

Princess Camomile.

Two wise men and their sister once passed the gates of a beautiful castle. It was built of red stone and the roof was built of red tiles. The windows were painted red and red curtains hung at every window.

'Who lives in such a beautiful castle?' said the first wise man to the second.

'The emperor and empress of this land,' replied the second.

'They must be very happy,' said the sister.

'Not at all,' retorted the second. 'For they are longing to have a child and so far it has proved impossible.'

'Then surely we could help them,' said the first man. 'If we told the empress to drink the dew gathered from the lily mixed with the dew gathered from the wormwood, then within one year she would give birth to a beautiful baby girl.'

'True,' replied the sister, 'but you must know that everything that is born of flowers must return to flowers, and when the time came the princess would have to return to the earth.'

'In that case,' said the first wise man, 'it is better that the empress does not know this, for her grief at such a sadness would surely kill her.'

So they all passed on, thinking that their secret was safe. But unknown to them they had been overheard by an old beggarwoman who immediately ran to the palace and told the empress that if she wished to have a child she should drink the dew gathered from the lily mixed with the dew gathered from the wormwood.

The empress was so pleased with the old lady's tidings that she gave her many precious gifts. But the beggarwoman did not tell the empress that her child would eventually return to the earth.

The empress commanded her maidservants to leave the palace early the next morning and bring to her dew collected from the lily and the wormwood. When the dews were brought to her, the empress mixed them together and drank.

Sure enough, within the year she gave birth to a beautiful baby girl. As the child grew she became more and more beautiful with every day that passed. But she was a solitary child and did not make many friends. As she grew older she spent more and more time walking in the palace gardens, talking to the flowers who replied in their own secret language. Her complexion became as white as the lilly and her hair smelled as sweetly as the wormwood that had given her life.

News of her beauty spread all over the kingdom and beyond.

Princes and kings travelled hundreds of miles to beg her to marry them, but to each one she said, 'I cannot marry you for I would only make you unhappy.'

She spoke so sincerely that all her suitors believed her and rode away with heavy hearts.

The emperor and empress began to worry about their daughter, for they knew that they would not live forever and they wanted to know that she would be well looked after when they were gone. One day the younger son of a neighbouring king rode up to the palace

Wow!
look at
that!
I didn't
do it
honestly.

to beg the princess to marry him. She gave him the same answer as she had to all the others. But he was persistent and no matter how often she told him that he would only be unhappy if he married her, he refused to take no for an answer. He demanded to know why she made such a sad prophecy. And the princess said, 'because the lily has told me that the moment I put on my wedding dress I will know that my time has come. And the wormwood has told me that as soon as I put wedding flowers in my hair, I will return to live amongst the flowers.'

At these words the prince laughed aloud and refused to believe such nonsense. He had such a friendly laugh and such a charming smile that the princess reluctantly agreed to be his bride.

The emperor and empress made preparations for the wedding with happiness in their hearts. The royal seamstress sewed a magnificent wedding gown for the lovely princess, and on the morning of the wedding when the guests began to arrive, the royal gardener picked the most beautiful blooms from the palace gardens and wove a bridal garland of such splendour that it has never been matched since.

When the princess put on the wedding gown she began to cry, for she knew then that what the lily said was true.

When she arrived at the chapel where her prince and all the guests were waiting, the gardener gave her the garland. As the princess put it on her head she closed her eyes for she knew that death was near. Sadly she walked up the aisle, to the sound of joyful music. Then suddenly the guests' happy smiles faded as they watched the deathly pale princess approach her bridegroom.

When she reached his side, he took her in his arms and gave her a tender embrace. Immediately the princess became a simple flower.

A few days later, the young prince rode sorrowfully home, the flower in his tunic. When he arrived at his father's palace he placed the flower in a vase and went to bed.

The next morning the single flower had turned into a huge bouquet of lovely blooms. He ordered his gardeners to plant some of them and a few months later his gardens were full of magnificent flowers. One day, a palace maid plucked some of the blooms and made an infusion from them. The liquid was so fragrant that when she washed her hair that evening, she added some of the flower water. When her hair had dried it shone like gold and smelled so sweetly. Ever since then fair-haired girls have washed their hair with the essence of the flower which was named after the sad princess – the daughter of the dew from the lily and the wormwood. Her name was Camomile.

Many hundreds of years ago, there was a young man who was an orphan. He lived with his grandmother and her three dogs.

In these days, there were no shops which sold food. The people had to hunt animals and search for berries in order to survive.

Although he was young, the man was an experienced hunter and killed many deer and bison with bow and arrow. In fact, he killed so many animals that at last the bison believed that if they were to survive at all they must kill him. So they called a council to decide how to do it. After much discussion, they thought of a plan. They knew that the youth was now of marriageable age and was eager to marry and have children. And so, using their magic powers, two of the bison changed themselves into beautiful young maidens.

The next evening they made their way to the youth's tent. As soon as the grandmother saw them, she was suspicious, for there was something in their faces she did not trust. The dogs, too, growled and barked when the two maidens approached the tent. The youth, however, was greatly impressed by their beauty. He ignored his grandmother's warnings and had the dogs tied up to a post, where they lay growling and whining far into the night.

The young man invited the maidens to eat with him and his grandmother, and when the supper was over he prepared a bed for them, insisting they must stay until daylight.

In the morning the maidens said to the young man, 'Won't you come home with us? We would like to repay your kindness with some gold which we have at home.'

'Do not go,' begged the grandmother, and something in her voice made the young man hesitate.

'At least go with us part of the way,' the maidens implored.

'Do not go unarmed,' warned the grandmother. 'Take your bow and arrows with you.'

And so the youth, armed with his bow and arrows set out with the two maidens. They walked for a few miles until they reached the plains where the herd of bison were waiting. As they approached the herd, the two maidens were transformed into the bison that they really were and instantly the whole herd surrounded the frightened youth. Suddenly he remembered his bow and arrows. He shot the first arrow into the ground where it magically changed into a tall poplar tree. Quickly the young man climbed into its branches, but the bison butted the tree with their horns and soon it began to fall to the ground where the herd were waiting. Then the youth took his second arrow and shot it into the ground beside the first. Immediately a second tree shot up, and as the first one fell, the youth jumped across and into its branches, where he thought he would be safe.

The bison butted the second tree and soon it too began to fall. The youth shot his third and fourth arrows into the ground and escaped in turn to the two trees that magically appeared. But the bison were determined to kill the youth and both the third and fourth trees were uprooted. In desperation the lad took his last arrow and shot it into the ground. The fifth arrow was thicker than the other four and the tree that sprang up where the arrow pierced the ground had a fine, thick trunk. The youth climbed to the topmost branches and taking up his hunting horn, he put it to his lips. He blew three strong blasts.

Far away, his three dogs heard the blasts and knew their master was in danger. They tugged and tugged at their tethers and eventually tore themselves free. Like the wind, they ran to their master, and in no time the charging bison had fled far away, never to be seen again.

And today, hundreds of years later, poplar trees still grow tall and straight and side by side in avenues where the hunter once fired his arrows into the ground.

DING DING
DING! DING! DING! DING!
TICK TOCK TICK TOCK
TICK TICK